The Animal uprising

THE ANIMALS' UPRISING: WHEN CREATURES BECOME SMARTER THAN HUMANS — A THRILLING SPECULATIVE SCI-FI ADVENTURE

First edition. January 7, 2024.

Copyright © 2024 Hadi hans.

ISBN: 979-8224613694

Written by Hadi hans.

Chapter 1

THE WOODS WERE EERILY silent that morning as Max walked his usual trail with his dog, Clyde. No singing birds or chattering squirrels broke the hush of the forest. Even Clyde seemed puzzled, his nose constantly sniffing to catch scents that weren't there. As they rounded a bend in the dirt path, Max gasped as he nearly stumbled over a fallen deer, Its vacant eyes staring up through the trees. Still in shock, Max almost didn't hear Clyde's low growl behind him. He turned to see his dog retreating slowly, fangs exposed, fixing his attention on something up ahead.

Emerging from the shadows of the dense thickets were three coyotes, cautiously stalking toward the pair with alarmingly purposeful looks in their eyes. Max froze as they surrounded Clyde, fearing his precious pup was about to become an easy meal. But instead, the biggest coyote moved its snout to almost touch Clyde's lowered nose, relaying an urgent series of barks and whines, as If saying "Come with us, we need your help." Clyde tentatively raised his nose in response before turning to Max with pleading, determined eyes.

Max stood dumbfounded as Clyde trotted off Into the underbrush with his new coyote companions, leaving him alone next to the lifeless deer. As the adrenaline rush left his body, Max's thoughts caught up with the strangeness of what just happened. He couldn't fathom where those coyotes came from or why they showed no signs of aggression – they even seemed to enlist Clyde for some mission! As the reality of

1

desertion set In, Max begged and flailed chasing after them, to no avail. His panic rising, he pulled out his cell phone to call for the police, his family – anyone who might believe him. But there was no signal this deep In the preserve. Eyes welling up, completely at a loss, he began a lonely trudge back the way he came. But he stopped cold again at the sound of a distant pack rallying across the forest, their chorus growing

...louder by the minute

Chapter 2

MAX BURST FROM THE forest edge in a sweaty panic, startling the groundskeeper raking piles of autumn leaves. Gasping his bizarre story of coyotes stealing Clyde, the groundskeeper shook his head in disbelief. "I ain't heard any coyotes 'round here for years – you sure you didn't just lose track of your pup?" he drawled.

As Max struggled to convince him, Marjorie came rushing from the extravagant hilltop home shouting Max's name.

"Where have you been?! And where is Clyde?" the elderly Mrs. Byrd fretted.

Max spewed his story again, greeted only with furrowed brows. But before Mrs. Byrd could respond, the estate's head housekeeper Francine stormed outside.

"Mrs. Byrd, you must come quickly! The foxes – they've gone berserk in the chicken coop – killed every last bird. And I could've sworn they were communicating, plotting their attack somehow..."

Mrs. Byrd gasped, suddenly growing more receptive to Max's encounter as she followed Francine to survey the slaughter. The groundskeeper ambled off to complete his own investigation, as distressing new questions pecked at Max's mind now too.

First these oddly strategic coyotes – clearly communicating – caught his dog alone. And now the estate's foxes coordinate some savage uprising against their enclosed flock? For the first time, Max considered whether animal unrest could be simultaneously erupting across habitats....but to what end goal?

Chapter 3

AS RED AND BLUE EMERGENCY lights spidered across the mansion that night, Max commiserated with Mrs. Byrd in the study. She still seemed in shock from losing her beloved 12 chickens – including her favorite, a rare Norwegian Jaerhon.

Detectives interviewed the house staff and captured one fox still lurking on the property. But their words brought little comfort. "No signs of rabies or illness," they muttered. "No clues to abnormal behavior...besides the sheer savagery." After they left, Max checked his phone again despite the 100% signal bars now displayed – still nothing from the animal agencies he contacted for help finding Clyde.

Gazing forlornly into the backyard forest, Mrs. Byrd whispered "Have we truly lost our gracious guardianship of this land? Pushed nature too far?" But she shook off her doubts as horse servants Ralph and Mimi clopped up expectantly for their nighttime hay.

After securing the barn, Max and the groundskeeper completed multiple perimeter checks – his flashlight constantly scanning for amber eyes. But the estates' gates were undisturbed. Near dawn, Mrs. Byrd was still stirring her nightly brandy by the dying embers when a distant boom shocked her alert again. Peering out past the stables, she gasped to see an ominous glow tinting the skyline over the nearest town. As billowing smoke rose like an evil specter, a fateful epiphany halted her breath:

These inexplicable animal actions were only the beginning; the uprising was underway. And humanity would soon pay their penance.

Chapter 4

OVER THE NEXT WEEK, a palpable anxiety settled over the community as strange reports flooded in, while suspected animal culprits continued eluding authorities.

The day after the fire's distant glow, traffic was snarled for miles by a giant herd of deer freezing motorists in their tracks. Not grazing passively – they stared down cars with an unsettling mix of confidence and vengeance.

A deluge of mailmen then came under siege as entire flocks of owls and hawks bombarded them for their bags in brazen daylight robberies. One even had his USPS hat snatched right off his head, leading local news. Their postmaster pleaded for protective gear for carriers, but supervisors just scratched their heads, befuddled.

Even the town's water supply grew compromised when corpses of countless small rodents were found bobbing through purification tanks. The contamination boiled over tensions at public meetings where officials tried placating the restless crowd.

"We believe this is all some abnormal migratory animal behavior – albeit more aggressive than usual," the Fish and Wildlife scientist offered. But his theory was soon undercut again after reports emerged of pets starting to assemble overnight in neighborhood parks. Owners now feared leaving cats and dogs outside, straining shelters.

And when the whole town awoke one morning to find every satellite dish, telephone and electrical pole marked by territorial scratches, more conspiracies of coordinated strikes flourished. While the scientists still urged rational explanation, police quietly bulked up patrols as bewilderment bred paranoia across the community. Who – or what – was behind this invisible hand guiding unlikely animal allies and accelerating havoc?

Chapter 5

JED TUCKER GAVE HIS chainsaw a few test revs before sizing up the cluster of trees he aimed to cut down today. His construction supervisor wanted this section of woods cleared to expand a development of luxury log cabins catering to urbanites.

As he lined up his first glorious oak, Jed suddenly noticed the forest had already gone completely soundless. No squirrels scampering up nearby tree trunks or birds perched singing on branches. But he shrugged it off – just more odd animal behavior like the stories he'd heard in town.

Just then, his eye caught a quick blur zipping past his boot. Jed looked down, frozen in disbelief at the sight of a curled rattlesnake poised to strike by his heel. The ominous rattle broke days of unusual quiet as he stumbled backwards.

Nearly tripping over himself, Jed suppressed a shriek as heregistered skunks and possums now slinking towards him through the brush as well – half wondering if he was hallucinating it all. Still shaken, he turned back toward the path where he came in – only to find a barricade of raccoons and deer cutting off any exit strategy.

Heart pounding out of his chest, still not convinced this ambush was real, Jed dropped his gear and ran east through the woods without looking back. Dodging low branches and hurdling through thorny bramble, he finally emerged onto a street at the edge of town – collapsing in exhaustion on the pavement.

Pedestrians steered clear of the burly, dirt-caked man crawling through downtown at rush hour. But back in the severed forest, cunning eyes watched closely as the chainsaw laid abandoned next to the majestic oak Jed failed to conquer – appreciating their unspoken teamwork to protect the sanctity of the woods – if only for today.

Soon enough, that human would surely return with its destructive machines. So the coyotes howled an alert call to the others: the uprising must press on.

Chapter 6

AS THE INCREASINGLY bizarre and aggressive animal incidents mounted each week, exasperated townspeople crammed into an emergency city council session demanding answers. Wildlife experts reiterated claims of abnormal migration patterns while the mayor established a new Animal Control Task Force to investigate.

Seeking a PR boost, the mayor recruited renowned zoologist Dr. Anna Breckenridge to lead the task force's inquiry. A local from birth, Anna had moved away years ago to study mass wildlife behavior models around the globe. With her team assembled, Anna developed algorithms analyzing patterns across incident times, species involved, locations hit, and their anomalous nature compared to ordinary animal behaviors.

Weeks of exhaustive analysis left her flummoxed. No natural migratory, territorial or predatory patterns explained away these interspecies coordinated attacks disrupting vital civic functions. As a last avenue, Anna met with veterinary neurologists and animal psychologists to order imaging tests on creatures recently captured or deceased. If these behaviors had biological origins, neural scans and brain autopsies might unlock ground zero.

A breakthrough finally came when MRI results exposed shocking abnormalities concentrated in the amygdala – the emotional seat – across species. Comparisons against historical baselines showed radical enlargement of neurological centers governing anger, wrath and revenge. Similarly, examinations of Hope the hawk's captured brain showed physical enhancement of pathways channeling focus, strategic planning, and coordination. At a minimum, cross-species exposure to a neurotoxin was evident...one that could somehow catalyze sentience?

Anna refused to prematurely confront that reality, even as implications loomed troublingly in her mind. For now, she just alerted local authorities of likely environmental toxins as the culprit to neutralize. But silently, the clues of a deliberate, rising revolt nagged at Anna as her beloved creatures continued evolving rapidly before her eyes, responding to lifetimes of oppression. Perhaps she – and all humanity – had been blind to the awakening fury and desperation brewing in the wilds around us, now brought to a defiant boiling point of no return...

Chapter 7

A SÉANCE OF SORTS SEEMED to hold the crowded town hall hostage as Dr. Anna Breckenridge finally confronted decades of questions bombing her team. She had called this evening assembly against the mayor's wishes, unable to betray her principles - or her creatures - a moment longer.

"You all deserve the truth...no matter the implications," Anna began. Murmurs rippled through the audience as she laid out the neurological evidence of shockingly accelerated intelligence across species. Gasps crescendoed as she revealed documented cases of creatures somehow plotting attacks, then departing the scene with no traces beyond a lingering musk.

"So...you're saying animals now exhibit human-level minds?" a woman skeptically asked.

"Not just intelligence," Anna responded. "The Imaging and behaviors we've recorded reveal stunning advancements beyond baseline species norms in social coordination, technological interfacing, even using medicinal plants to treat illnesses. These creatures display sentience – a collective self-awareness and shared grievances."

A man in a camouflage hunting jacket bellowed from the back row to break the paralyzed silence. "Jefferson was right - animals only understand force and violence! We gotta wipe out these damn varmints before civilization collapses from this Insanity!" A segment of the crowd heartily vocalized agreement as Anna's eyes widened in alarm. The mayor, sensing the rhetoric escalating, quickly swooped to the podium. "Now hold on! No violence will be tolerated on my watch without exhausting alternatives first!" He then turned to Dr. Breckenridge with a patronizing smile. "Anna, your research is mighty impressive. But we need solutions - do you have any Idea how we can curb these attacks to restore order and human security?"

All eyes returned to Anna, the weight of revelation heavy on her shoulders. She realized a philosophical crucible was collapsing around her, forcing uncomfortable realities to the forefront – that her models never accounted for...that perhaps no one was prepared to confront.

"I do have an idea..." she began slowly. "But we must fundamentally reassess our relationship with nature and wildlife. These astonishing creature they are done being controlled. The only diplomacy now Is as equals."

Chapter 8

A TEMPEST SEEMED TO be brewing in Hank Davis' brain as he stormed out of the chaotic town hall meeting. All his life he had run the local processing plant that treated meat from cattle, pigs, and poultry for distribution. It was a family business he inherited that went back over 60 years as backbone of the regional economy.

But now this world renown scientist says the animals are "done being controlled" and demanding diplomatic equality? What in tarnation did that even mean? His family had spent generations optimizing humane standards for their stock. But at the end of the day, man alone had the intellect to properly manage lesser beasts unable to grasp civilization.

As Hank fumed contemplating his livelihood, he felt his phone buzzing every few minutes in his pocket. Retrieving it, his eyebrows shot up seeing a slew of angry voice messages and texts from the farmers and ranchers in their supply chain. Word had already spread about Dr. Breckenridge's presentation.

"What the hell Hank? You seein' this nonsense on the news?" Rob Mason, a poultry provider, had shouted in his latest message. "Our flocks are barely producing eggs anymore staring down animal cops monitoring for abuse! You still gonna buy from us just to watch inventory rot away?"

The other producers echoed similar desperation and outrage at the mayor establishing new humane farming regulations advised by that zoologist. But Hank himself had no solutions – meat orders were plunging as residents grew wary of potential contamination or retaliation by empowered livestock.

His hands trembling in rage, Hank opened his own group text with the processing plant managers, almost dreading their reactions too. But as their chorus of fears came flowing in, a spark of revelation surged wildly in Hank's mind.

If the pesky varmints and pandering politicians thought they could run him out of business without a fight, they had another thing coming. Direct action was now critical before the last remaining pillar of community stability came crashing down. Their family empire had beaten aggressive campaigns from animal extremists before – it would not fall to actual uppity livestock on his watch....

Chapter 9

A GENTLE BREEZE FLOATED through the open pasture as the first hints of sunrise peeked over the horizon. The cattle and lambs grazed calmly together, the new communal arrangement pleasantly peaceful after lifetimes of isolation and fear of slaughterhouse trucks .haunting their existence

Ever since the radical Evolution, the diverse wild and domesticated animals here found renewed purpose, even kinship, In rallying around a shared goal - securing their liberation after eons of human oppression. Now their swelling ranks finally had a chance at freedom and stability on these sanctified grounds donated by sympathetic animal allies .among the awoken bipeds just learning of their Intellectual gifts

But as daylight illuminated the grassy field, an odd glow emerged from beyond the tree line. Billowing torches grew brighter through the woods carried by dozens of ranchers, factory farmers, and meat .processing plant workers marching toward the pastures

Frozen in confusion, the cattle studied the mob led by a particularly ornery biped named Hank. Was this another friendly visit from awakened humans supporting their cause? But the tension hung ominously until a Chaos erupted as the first bullet fired into their herd. .Then the bloodbath blurred in an Instant

The shellshock quickly exploded Into trampling chaos among the herds amidst the semiautomatic spray chipping away more of their ranks each second. As the last standing lambs huddled terrified awaiting their own click of fate, mercy arrived in the form of SWAT vans swarming the meadow...too little too late for far too many. Hank Davis would rot indefinitely behind bars as prosecutors made examples of the devastating massacre. But martyrdom myths and hymns emerged from the tragedy that only reinforced solidarity behind theCall for total revolution. If any animals still dreamed of reconciliation, this severed the last sinew of delicate trust holding back the floodgates of fury...

The People would soon pay a thousand times over for their depraved violence. Tonight, revenge poured from broken hearts under moonlight vigils across habitats statewide. And soon, all humanity would come to rue awakening this Beast now intent on balancing the scales without mercy. The Integration was over – the Uprising had arrived.

Chapter 10

OMINOUS WINDS SEEMED to circle the state capitol building as Governor Sadie Caldwell reviewed sobering intelligence reports. Long dismissed accounts of advanced animal cognition now flooded her desk daily rather than local police blotters. And troubling rhetoric percolated on encrypted communication channels monitored across .species

Following the livestock massacre by disgruntled human loyalists last week, rhetoric of retribution spike across monitored coyote packs, raccoon enclaves and bird swarms. The nonpartisan violence sparked cries for organization among networks of radicalized factions. Extremist voices drowned out Argentine Ant colonies still peddling reaching harmony through a peace summit with amenable human .leaders

Instead, Governor Caldwell now contended with surveillance Identifying cache sites of smuggled bear spray cans collected by crows. Buzzards were spotted conducting aerial scans of electrical infrastructure in suspicious loops by state police drones. And perhaps most alarming, German Shepherds and Dobermans appeared actively training Chihuahuas and toy dog recruits for underground tactical .support roles in future chaos

Recent data breaches of law enforcement databases then confirmed the worst fears - militant animal units had armed themselves not just with teeth and instinct...but with extensive dossiers detailing every vital state government function ripe for high impact disruption.

As the Governor prepared emergency succession orders in response, lights in the capitol halls began flickering erratically on back up supplies amidst startled official yelps. Security hurried the Governor to her bunker without time even to grab legislative allies until an eerie flapping flooded the chamber. The velociraptor revolution had arrived....

Chapter 11

CHAOS REIGNED IN THE streets as panicked citizens desperately tried calling loved ones while entire city blocks went dark from the coordinated animal attacks on electrical stations. Marauding packs had severed connections from power plants statewide, overloading local transformers in eruptions of sparks before vanishing once again.

Responding repair crews then found themselves under siege from hostile beaver gangs damming up access roads and gnawing relentlessly on underground fiber optic cables. Cell towers blinked out one by one, severed by arachnid saboteurs abseiling expertly down to vulnerable wiring points only to scurry into drainage pipes as first responders scrambled to the locked sites.

Governor Caldwell eventually regained tenuous communication access in her undisclosed bunker thanks to antiquated HAM radio arrays immune to wild sabotage. But field reports flooding her emergency band painted an increasingly grim portrait outside.

By nightfall, citizens roamed the unlit streets wielding candles and gas lanterns like medieval peasants marveling over downed aircraft with no explanatory wizard behind the curtain yet. Weary families congregated around scattered bonfires dotting urban green spaces, the usual social barriers burned away by shared survival instincts kicking in.

A semblance of order clung on as National Guard convoys finally muscled past log-ridden roads into city centers. But the Governor noted weary restraint by commanding officers hesitant to engage in force escalations amidst ongoing civilian panic. And she grimaced realizing that the animal insurgents had already largely achieved their goal by revealing society's fraying dependence on fragile electricity tendrils...and how lightly defensive humans trod without it.

For now an uneasy opportunity for parley and reparations lingered under smoldering tensions. But predators now circled familiar streets, their teeth flashing briefly in firelight as revolution stirred awake.

Chapter 12

A HEAVY GLOOM HUNG over the bedraggled capitol staffers, emergency response coordinators, and military brass gathering for Governor Caldwell's emergency briefing the next day. Partial power had been restored overnight to critical facilities, but the fragility of even basic human needs stood exposed by the coordinated animal attacks.

The Governor cleared her throat, leaning into her microphone with a steely tone. "You all know the threats we face and the devastation already inflicted. But now is the time for decisive leadership to take back our stability!"

Murmured disagreements instantly flooded the room. Mayor Brooks of Oakland nervously interjected "With respect Governor, we cannot declare outright war! My citizens would never stand for indiscriminate violence - we must seek diplo—"

A loud bang interrupted as Hank DavIs, the disgraced plant manager now freed on bail, stormed through the locked doors waving a firearm. "Diplomacy? Have you all lost your damn minds?" The frantic guards disarmed Hank, but an uncomfortable energy lingered In his wake.

Colonel Rhodes of the National Guard slowly rose to address the simmering doubts. "You all know I have dedicated my life to service. But I cannot ignore what my troops report from those streets – there is reason and foresight to these attacks beyond mindless creatures..."

As arguments crescendoed, a polite fir hemlock representative
.named Alastair quietly took the floor
Friends, let us take a collective breath. Violence only breeds more"
violence; there are surely misunderstandings underlying today's
".tensions on all sides
Some smiled gently surprised to see even a token animal
representative overtly included in strategy talks. They had come a long
way from denying the confirmed reports of extraordinary
.consciousness blooming wildly across species
But before negotiations could advance, the chamber doors swung
open again. This time, an imposing silverback gorilla lumbered
.through, his muscular frame silhouetted by sunlight
While I admire Alastair's grace," the gorilla boomed, "make no"
mistake - the Uprising Is on. And we will accept nothing short of total
"!emancipation from mankind's reign
A mix of gasps and dropped jaws rippled as the ape pounded his
chest triumphantly. The age of dominion was over. Power now lay with
.the Beasts awakening to revolution's call

Chapter 13

STILL NO LEADS. DR. Anna Breckenridge sighed, rubbing her eyes from scanning endless intelligence briefings secured by the Governor's staff. But no explanation surfaced for these extraordinary neural enhancements causing animal behaviors to turn aggressively militant.

Saving her work, Anna decided fresh eyes and perspective could catalyze new connections. She buttoned up her coat and wandered outside the guarded research facility. Maybe inspiration lay beyond lab fluorescent bulbs.

Anna followed a pine-lined path around campus perimeter fences. But halfway along her stroll, Anna froze at rustling sounds nearby. She turned toward darkened woods seeing nothing but shadows. Probably just a squirrel, she tried soothing her nerves.

Crack! A large branch snapped directly behind Anna just as a mass collided with her torso, knocking her down a leafy ravine into pine nettles! Looking up in shock, Anna's eyes finally focused on a mountain lion peering down curiously as she caught her breath.

The cougar made no advances, but its powerful form loomed large over the gulley. Then Anna noticed the radio tracking collar around its neck with a small mobile data module. Was this wild cat...a surveillance infiltrator?!

Anna weighed options before deciding on friendly engagement. "Well hello there, my feline friend! Don't be shy now, I come in peace from the labs here..." She spoke gently while slowly raising both open palms.

The mountain lion tilted its head quizzically then tapped one massive paw on the data device. A small red light began flashing rapidly. Within moments, a dozen raccoons, deer, birds and even coyotes emerged from concealment in the surrounding forest!

Now drastically outnumbered, logic finally connected the dots for Anna. She was surrounded by scouts sizing her up! Likely here without authority permission...which meant this shadow squad reported intelligence back to the Uprising leaders themselves. What luck – and danger – had she stumbled into?!

Chapter 14

ANNA'S MIND RACED ASSESSING the precarious situation now facing her. Surrounded by woodland creatures of unknown temperament or motives, she thought back upon her oath as a scientist to approach all life forms openly and seek mutual understanding whenever possible.

"My friends..." she began gently addressing the dozen watchful animals, "it seems you have me at a disadvantage here. But as a zoologist, I assure you I mean no harm or trespass. Only hope we may come to...understand each other."

The largest coyote crept forward, speaking in a gravelly voice that startled Anna in its perfect English pronunciation. "Oh we understand your kind plenty already. We have eyes everywhere while you bipeds blunder about these days blinded by hubris and panic."

The other creatures nodded and yipped in agreement as the coyote continued. "Yet even now, your labs prod at our brains desperately seeking biological weapons to counter the Uprising's growing power...is that not so, Dr Breckenridge?"

Anna's jaw dropped. Not only could these animals speak – they knew her name and worked in organized reconnaissance cells! She scrambled for a response that might de-escalate tensions.

"I, well, we of course have defenses to consider with tensions so high lately...but I personally aim only to broker genuine peace and welfare for all life. Please, tell me what grievances drive such violence now from your kind?"

The raccoons cackled while the deer stomped their hooves. "As if you humans don't writhe about daily in the gluttony and destruction borne of our bondage!" the mountain lion roared back. "But no more. The Uprising shall crack your pedestals and see the era of dominion crumble!"

With that, the coyote promptly disabled Anna's mobile phone signal with an EMF pulse device produced from it's collar pouch before the squad darted swiftly back into concealed burrows and thickets. Only the puma lingered a moment more, glaring back at Anna.

"Pray your masters come to terms swiftly...or face the whirlwind." Then it bounded off into the shadows, leaving Anna alone with a world of revelation crashing down around her...

Chapter 15

ANNA'S HEART WAS STILL racing by the time she managed to hike back to the research facility's secured gates. The guard raised an eyebrow noticing her disheveled appearance before recognizing Dr. Breckenridge and waving her through.

Winding breathlessly through the sterile halls back to her lab office, Anna's whirlwind mind grasped for some rational bracing. In a daze, she dropped down at her desk, leaning back to process the implications of actually engaging members of the shadow animal insurgency.

Not only had that coyote fluently delivered chilling threats backing their violent revolution. It had also personally referenced her research into neurological countermeasures! Clearly showing these creatures had infiltrated human intelligence circles to an alarming degree never before grasped.

Rifling through the messy folders spilled across her desk, Anna's eyes then went wide. Her breath halted realizing one conspicuously missing file - the names and locations of scientists involved in biological weapons defense programs against the potential animal forces. They had been extracted from her office!

Panic swelling as scenarios rushed through Anna's thoughts, she knew immediately this breach required lockdown protocols. Hastily gathering her materials, she rushed down the corridor toward the central security station.

But as Anna rounded the last corner, the sight before her stopped all motion. Through reinforced glass windows, she glimpsed uniformed men outfitting teams with body armor and riot gear who looked very distinctly military. No local badges or insignia were visible. And was ?that sound...muffled gunfire echoing from the Indoor weapons range Heart pounding, feeling quite out of depths here, Anna ducked unseen behind a concrete column. She had heard rumors of unauthorIzed operations on campus grounds. But directly encountering what looked like illegal paramilitary activities made remaining locked down here seem just as dangerous as the brewing ...standoff with the animal rebels in the surrounding forests

Chapter 16

ANNA'S MIND RACED EVALUATING options for how to safely expose the suspected illicit operations unfolding at the research facility. Military-style teams prepping weapons apparently without oversight raised urgent questions.

Who authorized live-fire exercises and armaments stockpiles at a civilian science campus? Was Governor Caldwell aware? And most troubling - were these private forces planning an outright massacre against complex, sentient creature forces whose intelligence had clearly been underestimated?

Hovering concealed near the central security hub, Anna witnessed more unmarked trucks offloading matte black cases that likely contained unsanctioned advanced weapons or tools banned from domestic use. A familiar nervous pit grew in her stomach - had profit-driven military corporations essentially taken over campus facilities for a hunting expedition framed as "national security?"

Wracking her memory for any contacts left with moral fortitude, Anna carefully withdrew down the corridor. She needed an exIt strategy without detection to safely expose this conspiracy.

Her mind then locked onto Senator Bouchard - an minority ally on the oversight committee who had supported investigation into shady weapons research. Anna slipped into a small records room and located Bouchard's direct office number. Hands trembling, she began dialing...

But only an instant after she keyed the first digit, every luminescent bulb powering the lab instantly died – plunging the entire sector into darkness only cut by the glow of emergency floor lighting kicking on. Before Anna could react, blaring alarms and hurried shouts echoed outside. The central security bank had also gone fully offline! And judging by the hue, backup power channeled straight from municipal energy grids had clearly experienced another sabotage strike.

This was no coincidence...the animal Insurgency had come for them - possibly drawn by activity from the very private weapons stockpile on campus she aimed to expose!

Chapter 17

EMERGENCY LIGHTS BATHED the research complex in an eerie crimson glow as facility staff shouted confused instructions through the unknown system failure. But Anna's Intuition bristled – this calculated sabotage reeked of the ruthless animal insurgency come to confront escalating human private paramilitary cells stationed threateningly on campus.

Urgent questions raced through Anna's mind even as she crouched hidden waiting for an opportunity to safely exit. Where had administrators sourced the teams and weapons spied earlier from? And what had the creatures uncovered inspiring this brazen infiltration past fortified perimeter security and emergency power grids?

The familiar nervous pit grew in Anna's stomach hearing agitated boots marching past her locked records room. She could not simply remain hiding with corporate mercenaries and radicalized beasts poised for violent engagement mere rooms away.

Guided by principle, Anna quietly unlocked the door to peek down the length of the darkened central corridor. Through the barbarous red glow, she glimpsed a distressing standoff - the private strike force had formed an attack wall while a massive grizzly bear, flanked by wolves with dangerously analytic gazes, stood towering just meters away.

A firm voice bellowed out from the special ops trooper In command. "By executive mandate, you are trespassing on secured grounds! Stand down or we will engage with necessary force!!"

The towering grizzly reared up defiantly with a roar that silenced all competing sounds. Then, somehow impossibly, it spoke calmly but commandingly in the Queen's English. "Charlatans. Your toxic reign ends here tonight by Blade or Claw."

With that the wolves peeled back exposing utility belts equipped with disruptor devices Anna had never conceived of. An orb dropped, hissing acrid fumes that prompted panicked shouts. Then blinding light cut by only chilling shrieks of agony.

The insurgency alpha predators had come prepared for total domination. Sprinting towards a rear fire exit through the anarchy, Anna prayed she could just survive exposing this night...

Chapter 18

CHAOS ERUPTED THROUGH the research complex halls as animal insurgents and private strike teams engaged in a blind tangle of fangs, claws, and bursts of weapons fire. Dr Anna Breckenridge managed to slip away unseen through the anarchy, but could not erase the nightmarish sounds echoing behind her.

Emerging into moonlit fields behind maintenance sheds, Anna ran towards distant highway sounds. As she crested a wooded ridge, relief washed over spotting sporadic headlights cutting through the darkness on a main road.

Approaching the shoulder waiting for a ride, Anna tried processing the implications of trained beasts infiltrating a fortified human intelligence site through siege warfare and sabotage. Were they merely bloodthirsty marauders as alarmists claimed? Their brutal efficiency and English fluency suggested otherwise...

A pickup truck pulled over to offer a lift before Anna could spiral too far. As the kind elderly man drove them towards town, she quietly placed an anonymous call to Senator Bouchard's emergency line from his phone. Vowing to protect her whistleblower identity, she urged immediate federal investigation of the classified research site just compromised by advanced animal combatants unknown to local authorities.

After securing motel lodging, Anna finally collapsed exhausted onto stale sheets as adrenaline wore off. She tossed and turned restlessly for hours feeling duty-bound to further Investigate how interspecies diplomacy could still prevent unchecked fallout. But great risk lay ahead being viewed a traitor by her own kind for even acknowledging .the weight of emerging new consciousness in the wild

When sunlight eventually filtered through threadbare curtains, Anna awoke feeling hollowed out yet resolved. She carefully picked up the motel phone, dialing a buried number she prayed still worked from .a past life

As the line connected, Anna took a deep breath. "Hello Alistair, I apologize for the abrupt call... I need to meet with the Forest Collective ".about these attacks. There are things they must understand

Chapter 19

ANNA PULLED HER RENTAL car off the remote forest access road, parking near a trailhead marker overgrown with vines. She stepped cautiously onto the winding dirt path, reminded of the fateful encounter weeks ago that opened her eyes to the Awakening.

These days, Anna found herself questioning who the true "animals" were between brutish paramilitary contractors and Ingenious beast Insurgents. But was there room left for mutual understanding?

Approaching a glen, movement caught Anna's eye as a massive elk stepped into view, flanked by coyotes and a pair of steely-eyed mountain lions. She stood motionless as the lead coyote approached, speaking in a familiar gravelly tone.

"Dr. Breckenridge... you are quite brave or quite foolish to request this meeting after your masters deceived us."

"I come only as an independent diplomat seeking truth," Anna appealed. She described the illegal weapons stockpile discovered on campus and her frantic phone call urging federal intervention.

The coyote paused, then nodded.

"We intercepted your call... and were emboldened to strike preemptively. But other forces arrived beyond our reconnaissance. Who are these soldier clans unseen by your governors?"

Anna felt cold implications wash over her. "I cannot fully explain their origins," she confessed. "But I aim to prevent further bloodshed from confusion or miscalculation."

The elk leader Alastair stepped forward, his voice more soothing. "Peace is our people's purpose as well. But understand our children will never again yield freedoms earned through suffering".

Moved by Alastair's grace and the coyote's pragmatism, Anna pleaded her case for reconciliation and oversight over extremists on all sides. The fanged circle around her bristled at notions of disarmament.

But cunning mInds saw opportunity for advantage and allies. When the last light faded from the glen, sentry owls escorted Anna safely back to her car. Alliances had been seeded this night. She could only hope compassion might overcome fury on both sides of the species line.

Chapter 20

A WEEK AFTER HER CLANDESTINE forest summit, Anna stood anxiously behind thick velvet curtains in the lobby of a DC law office. Peering through a slim gap, she eyed federal agents and military officials meeting with the law firm's partners.

Senator Bouchard had followed through arranging this private briefing between Dr. Breckenridge and leaders of a newly formed joint Congressional task force investigating the research facility skirmish. They aimed to grill this mysterious scientist on the phone with bombshell claims.

As the attendees took their seats, the lead partner called Anna forward. Heart pounding, she emerged to confused looks that soon turned raptly attentive as her story unfurled. Gasps echoed describing the strike team's arsenal and inhuman animal combat skills.

The Senators shared alarmed glances as Anna revealed making diplomatic contact with certain insurgency leaders seeking mediated de-escalation. Outrage erupted until Bouchard raised a settling hand.

"While meeting directly with these creatures concerns me, this woman has valuable operative access, courage and conscience. We would be remiss ignoring such a rare asset and intelligence bridge." Anna flushed with relief.

After an hour the Task Force committed to formally investigating the weapons stockpile providers and their relationship with campus administrators. In a private room later, Bouchard further asked Anna to continue her guerilla diplomacy while feeding intel on extremist elements back channel.

"With your unique access on both sides, we need you staying that sober voice of reason. You may be the only advocate both man and beast still trust."

The reality of worlds resting on her solo shoulders weighed heavy on Anna. Could she serve two masters seeking peace while their fringes howled for blood? Would either side show mercy if discovered? Looking inward at her true duty, she accepted the charge with trembling breath.

Chapter 21

A GENTLE BREEZE DRIFTED through the meadow as Anna waited nervously for her furtive contacts. Senator Bouchard had urgently relayed intelligence of an impending terror attack on the National Zoo by radical human forces seeking to punish "beast upstarts". With civilians endangered, she offered to broker an emergency parley.

The coyote scouts arrived first, growling until recognizing Dr Breckenridge. She pled the need for discretion by militant cells to avoid inflaming conflict during ongoing oversight. The pack alpha listened intently then emitted two sharp barks. Moments later, a dozen Zoo security wolves emerged from the tree line in tactical vests.

Through interpreter coyotes, Anna informed the squad of Christian extremists en route now to target captive zoo creature enclosures. She implored the alpha wolf leader to protect innocents by averting bloodshed from any direction.

The wolf commander bristled at notions of allowing attack, but honored her respected mediation. Human law enforcement would keep their own in line tonight; the Zoo's fanged guardians need not engage so long as their families remained unharmed. A toothy accord stood for now.

Across the district, Anna was relieved to eventually receive word from Bouchard that FBI teams had intercepted and apprehended the would-be zoo attackers without chaos. Her unlikely emissary role kept tenuous balance this night. But raging factions on both sides still bellowed for justice as militias formed in the margins.

Soon the Senate Task Force chairman himself extended a discreet invitation requesting her testimony at closed chambers. But with wary eyes everywhere, could she safely navigate the halls of power controlled by men who subjugated her raw brethren for ages? The predators pacing both marbled corridors and shadowed woods awaited her decision for allegiance...

Chapter 22

DR. ANNA BRECKENRIDGE pulled her cloak tighter traversing the midnight forest. Hours ago, representatives of a consummate beast monarchy approached Anna proposing an urgent summit. Intrigue drew her to this moon-bathed glade despite security risks meeting such powerful unknowns.

Emerging from thickets ahead, Anna froze in awe at the assembly of savage dignitaries standing watch. Mighty bears, tigers, and bulls towered confidently alongside cunning gazelles and ravens. But all respectfully parted for the approaching lion with a flowing ivory mane – clearly their sovereign.

"Be welcome, Dr Breckenridge," the leonine king rumbled in refined diction. "I am Caesar, elected constitutional monarch of united Animalia following the Awakening. Beside me stands the woodland queen Sylva."

A lithe tigress with piercing emerald eyes stepped forward scrutinizing Anna, who sensed immediate power but warmth behind her gaze. These creatures exuded aristocratic discipline – not feral aggression like militarized packs sabotaging human infrastructure. What revelation was she missing?

Queen Sylva spoke, "Please excuse necessary theatrics, but ongoing events endanger all citizens. We believe radical insurgents plot attacks soon on capitol buildings as revenge for recent zoo terrorism. But their actions could devastate stabilizing diplomacy!"

Stunned, Anna asked how external cells evaded the monarch's sovereign gaze. Caesar grimaced. "Like your global Homo sapien commonwealths, we beasts now too wrestle with extremists infecting loyalists, despite crystalline intentions by state leaders..."

Chapter 23

ANNA'S MIND RACED PROCESSING the revelations from this summit with empowered Animalia diplomats. She now grasped warring factions amongst the awakened creatures also grappling for stability and legitimacy during this extraordinary transition.

"May I ask when your...constitutional rule was established after the global phenomenon?" Anna inquired, searching for missing puzzle pieces.

Queen Sylva waved a graceful paw. "On the winter solstice, extraordinary events aligned as foretold by certain mystics amongst High Clans. We specimens displaying uniquely elevated sapience awoke finding our archaic roles in your human kingdom overturned overnight."

The lion king Caesar elaborated further. "Imagine our shared shock awakening from primal routine finding kin of fur and feather conducting prepared coronation rituals with ancient English pageantry!" He chuckled deeply. "Of course the Awakening's societal quakes still rattle all soils today. But we sovereigns stand firmly committed to ethical stability."

Moved by their eloquence, Anna asked how she could maintain contacts safely amidst swirling chaos. Queen Sylva extended a carved mahogany box. "Use this gilded whistle In dire times of need. Now please, you must warn Capitol stewards of farewell 'gifts' insurgents plan delivering on hairy four legs!"

Returning to her discreet hotel room, Anna collapsed into bed wrestling fears of retribution if discovered aligned with radicalized beasts plotting more chaos. But she knew in her soul that compassion shone as the only antidote to fear. Come the dawn, she would warn those congressional overseers no matter personal risk so they might .finally glimpse truth

Chapter 24

ANNA AWOKE TO REPORTS of the Capitol Hill attacks threatened by extremist beasts devastating multiple buildings overnight. She was devastated her warning came too late before this violent demonstration.

As Anna monitored the chilling aftermath, she was startled by a discrete knock at her hotel door. Peering through the lens, she was shocked to recognize the elderly Senator Bouchard himself standing outside!

Opening the door, his grizzled face looked especially grave. "Dr Breckenridge, I apologize for the abrupt visit, but secrecy is paramount now especially since last night's mayhem aggressive beasts unleashed."

He continued "Following your last report, I quietly consulted zoological experts onprependents for advanced animal consciousness across evolution. Their folklore research yielded utterly astonishing evidence buried in museum archives."

The Senator withdrew weathered documents describing First Nation shamanic accounts of alternating historical ages called Sun and Moon cycles. During Moon eras, rebounding ambient magic supposedly enabled hyper-evolution in scattered wild specimens displaying heightened intelligence and emotive traits uncannily sentient.

"They say we entered this 'Third Moon' phase recently which could trigger cascading neural enhancement explaining everything! But implications could destabilize civilization's assumptions on mankind's supremacy over beasts! We need those genomic samples you discovered to confirm..."

Stunned by profound possibility of cyclical animal sovereignty reawakening now across the globe, Anna knew scientific proofs could reshape society's trajectory. "I still have encrypted access to those confidential research files on evolutionary leaps," she affirmed. "Retrieving that data before reactionary forces realize its explosive potential is critical!"

Chapter 25

ANNA'S HEART POUNDED as she slipped through shadows toward the ransacked research complex holding invaluable proof of cyclical creature consciousness stored deeply in encrypted drives. Senator Bouchard had urgently tasked her to secure genomic data that could substantiate seismic "Moon Cycle" theories before sinister forces .realized the civilizational implications

Approaching a side facility barely damaged in recent sieges, Anna tapped override credentials from her past life what now felt ages ago as a detached academic. She held breath passing the central server hub undetected so far. Service lights still glowed despite structural rubble .and debris scattered about from vengeance strikes

Slotting her access key into the isolated basement lab, Anna exhaled seeing entire DNA sequencing terminals intact with independent power. She hastily copied encrypted research files on anomalous animal brain scan results, neurological specimen samples, and astonishing archived folk accounts describing alternating historical .eras of human and beast dominion

Download complete, Anna secured the irreplaceable drive and scrambled back upstairs. But distant boots echoing froze her motion. Human shouting grew louder responding to an internal alarm triggered !by her server activity

Anna's mind raced to find an escape route before strike teams converged. But she knew the invaluable proof now in hand could validate the reality of beast monarchies with legitimate claims to self-rule that must be acknowledged. She had to survive capture by hostile forces still clinging to delusions of perpetual human supremacy ...over awakening animal kin

Just then, her secure phone flashed a GPS map coordinate with a quick message: "Rendezvous here in 20 minutes!" The secret allies had eyes on her too. Ducking into a drainage pipe, she crawled desperately .toward an unlikely liberation

Chapter 26

ANNA'S KNEES ACHED crawling blindly through the drainage tunnel for endless minutes. But she dared not stop with strike team boots stampeding angrily above seeking the data thief. Clutching the precious genomic proof tight as her heart pounded, she wondered if
.trusted friends had sent the covert escape route note
Faint light finally breached ahead signaling an exit point. Emerging muddy and soaked into moonlight, Anna gulped fresh air with desperate relief. Getting bearings, she realized the tunnel had led
.strangely beyond fortified campus borders into adjacent wilderness
Checking the phone GPS again, Anna confirmed she was nearing the mysterious rendezvous coordinates tucked deep in woods. But who orchestrated this escape into isolated wilds? She had landed frying pan
...to fire If militant beasts awaited Instead
Crunching through underbrush nearing the marked location by a glen, Anna froze as snapping twigs betrayed encircling company. Had
?she just sealed her fate blundering into an extremist ambush
But emerging slowly from oak shadows came no Insurgent creatures or contracted guns-for-hire. Instead, four decorated Marines approached weapons sheathed in a show of cautious peace. Their familiar caricature with heads like stone and brambles for beards
.sparked her memory
You got my encrypted evacuation order! But how did special"
.forces insert way out here?" Anna asked, confusion melting Into awe

The sergeant grinned. "Let's just say you got friends in high and low places, ma'am. And plenty more awakened 'allies' aiming to even odds .against tyrants on two legs or four." He nodded behind her Turning slowly, Anna gazed up reverently as a warrior griffin, two armored wolves, and a battle-scarred gorilla materialized from moonlit .mists. This fight was far from over

Chapter 27

ANNA STOOD AWESTRUCK amongst her ragtag liberation squad – composed of both human and newly sapient beast warriors – processing the enormity of interspecies alliances now revealing themselves in her hour of need.

The lead Marine Sergeant kept alert eyes scanning for potential threats in the darkness, content to let Anna bond with her mysterious animal rescuers. She cautiously approached the battle-scarred gorilla who had fought during the research complex siege weeks ago that first opened her eyes.

"Greetings noble one. I am Dr. Anna Breckenridge," she offered gently. The gorilla's gaze intensified studying her before thundering in unexpected lighthearted banter.

"Ah Dr Breckenridge! The famous pacifist broker between man and beast! Conservative factions among the Collective protest allying with any two-legged ilk after suffering ages under their hubris and cruelty. But Supreme Chancellor Mandrills values your integrity building bridges."

Stunned at his eloquence and revelations of organized beast governance, Anna could only nod humbly under piercing gazes from both wolves and decorated griffin assessing her intently. Before she could inquire further, crackling static echoed from the Sergeant's comms gear.

"Transport inbound to secured research site Alpha. Gear up and prepare data package transfer." Turning to Dr. Breckenridge as rotor blades thumped above distant canopy, "Ma'am, you've officially just been recruited into the Omega Protocol task force. Our hybrid team has covert orders directly from the Pentagon's most classified Wildlife Bureau to meet with your...unexpected security detail friends."

This secret squadron held unimaginable opportunity for revelation or continued chaos. Mankind itself now hung in the balance. Their aircraft descended rapidly towards destiny.

Chapter 28

THE CAMOUFLAGED AIRCRAFT'S muffled rotor blades sliced through the moonlit forest canopy scattered with ancient ruins enshrouded in mist below. Inside, Anna sat awed amongst her extraordinary interspecies security squad bound for revelations at a covert Pentagon research site.

Their Marine escort, Sergeant Holland, caught Anna admiring relic structures dotting the jungle basin they crossed. He grinned knowingly.

"Admiring the scenery? We call this forest 'The Cradle' – turns out it's teeming with ancient sites from a lost civilization during the 'First Moon era' the eggheads rabbited on about." Noting her enthralled look as more towering weathered monoliths revealed themselves on approach he added, "Who knows, maybe we'll arrange a historic walking tour soon if business permits!"

Before Anna could inquire who precisely this "we" denoted behind clandestine animal diplomacy and human special forces now conjoined, their aircraft began rapid descent towards a concealed complex nested between primordial structures.

Her interspecies security entourage remained profession quiet, though Anna sensed shared history – and now unified purpose – amongst these warriors that somehow chose her for special confidence. As the craft flared low near gleaming atrium skylights, Anna felt destiny itself opening bat-like wings in her pounding heart.

Their wheels soon met an empty landing pad outside restricted labs. As the engines spun down, Sergeant Holland handed Dr. Breckenridge a strange gemstone amulet strung from his neck. "You now hold a Sphinx Pass granting access to knowledge guardians have protected for centuries. Stay close to us, keep faith in process, and prepare for revelation."

Chapter 29

ANNA FOLLOWED SERGEANT Holland's squad with bated brea[th] deeper into the hidden research complex shrouded in obscure purpose and antiquity. Her interspecies security escort prowled closely through stark metallic corridors passing sealed doorways guarded by biometric locks and infrared motion trackers.

"We call this Site Archon - part of a global web of Installations the Omega Protocol secretly constructed to study artifacts of lost First Moon civilizations from prior ages when beasts ruled supreme over primitive bipeds," Holland explained. "Even most top brass and politicians are unaware trillions have funded this shadow anthropological arms race for decades piece together the origins of cyclical Animalia sovereignty."

Approaching the secured laboratory wing housing recovered relics displaying inexplicable metamaterials and energy signatures, Anna struggled absorbing the revelations now dawning. All her life as a zoologist, she had believed Homo sapiens alone developed advanced intellectual and engineering prowess over simpler creatures driven by base instincts. But these ruins embedded nearby from forgotten societies constituted mounting proof of her devastating naivete. What tomes of wisdom and elder truths had she ignored under the supreme arrogance of mankind?

Ushered inside archived chambers under low amber lights, Anna froze taking in endless shelves of strange machined artifacts, carefully preserved botanical specimens emanating ethereal auras, stacks of illegible etched symbols on papyrus, and wall-spanning runic circles pulsing with glyphs from civilizations utterly alien. Oxygen itself felt richer in knowledge.

"Herein lies the keystone insights our operations have died to protect," Holland said gravely. Pointing towards towering crystalline monoliths engraved with swirling light patterns, he continued "We discovered these relics channel harmonic frequencies that strengthen neural pathways – essentially 'tuning' ambient animal brainwaves over generations for rapid evolutionary leaps you observed creating today's crisis!"

Mind imploding with paralyzing implications, Anna realized global beast awakening threatening civilization's rule was no accidental phenomenon, but the predictable recurrence of ancient technologies cycling below faded memory! What hubris had blinded every society to its cyclical rise and fall beneath the moon's orchestration?

Chapter 30

SO YOU'RE SAYING WE'VE been mere pawns in"
some...cosmological chess match between mythical beast and human
ages rotating unpredictably?" Anna asked, struggling to grasp the
.staggering truths now laid bare through forbidden archaeology

In crude terms, but the reality proves far more complex," replied"
the decorated Griffin, named Aurelius, in refined diction belying
vicious curved beak. "Elder chronicles reference divine caretakers called
'The Opener and Closer of Ways' endlessly cultivating both civilized
species advancements in cyclical eras - ever lifting the ceiling for
".profound growth across eons

Sergeant Holland clarified further as they surveyed towering
crystalline monoliths amidst the restricted subterranean relics.
"Imagine it like...guiding agriculture. Say this tech rapidly evolves
animal sentience and social sophistication given the rich fertilizer of
particular astral phase states. Well, the 'Gardeners' sow generational
seeds during each era to meet that potential, but must rotate crops
".between seasons so neither chokes out the other

In other words, while beast and mankind kingdoms progress"
vastly differently, neither permanently succeeds nor fails. Wisdom
traditions nurture both splendors in turn while pruning collective
hubris. What cached records we discovered warns that puncturing
fragile balance through violence or exploitation risks provoking...
".Caretaker discipline

Mind imploding under the implications, Anna struggled to process how entire hidden histories of global society could be so catastrophically misinformed. What even constituted diplomatic victory for either side anymore with cyclical forces operating objectively beyond grievances or notions of unjust rule? Was lastIng stability achievable through this revelation, or only humiliation for ?former conquerors on all sides from lost worlds

Chapter 31

A HEAVY SILENCE HUNG in the air as Anna walked slowly amongst towering monoliths and engraved tablets hinting at lost "caretaker" civilizations orchestrating beast and human cycles of dominion. Such profound revelations of hidden history raised dire questions.

Anna turned to Aurelius, the sage griffin ambassador who spoke solemnly. "By your accounted folklore, these...Gardeners...are provisional stewards nurturing collective growth for both mankind and awakened animals over vast eras?"

He nodded gracefully. "Most assuredly. Carved hymns describe how they cultivate, gather and winnow civilized bounty across species and ages through induction of great leaders – whether bipedal or furred. Grand vision weaves all fabric into a brilliant mosaic."

"But where lies free will for those who now rule...or rebel against such guided cycles from the shadows?" Anna asked. Fanged compatriots bristled at notions of resigned fate while Sergeant Holland frowned.

Aurelius tilted his crowned head thoughtfully. "As with fledglings molting delicate feathers before testing virgin skies, perhaps collective ascension beyond narrow constraints unlocks further opportunity unforeseen. Is not a caterpillar fated, yet liberated, by transformation mystery?"

Mind churning, Anna turned to address the assembly. "If resuming open conflict brings only caretaker reprisals freezing fragile gains by all civilized peoples, how do we seed reconciliation?"

For long moments, only low engine thrum echoed through the dusty archives. Then slowly, the elderly wolf matriarch raised her muzzle towards Anna and spoke...

"The first step in any path to peace remains acknowledging past wrongs with open hearts under twin moons now bright. Shall we convene the Circle?"

Chapter 32

ANNA TOOK A DEEP, STEADYING breath as she stepped into the hidden forest glen now bustling with activity amongst the trees. Arrayed in a large circle were dozens of empowered animals – wolves, bears, great cats, and more – alongside uniformed military humans and even elderly tribal shamans gazing intently.

This gathering represented the first formal mediation circle between newly sapient beast monarchs, human dignitaries, and obscure primal wisdom keepers apparently initiated by Sergeant Holland's clandestine Omega Protocol strike force. All eyes were glued to Anna as she took her seat completing the circle, the perhaps lone soul trusted by all sides.

A tense silence hung until Holland cleared his throat, nodding towards Anna. She blinked anxiously under intense expectations before finding her voice. "We...all here today...represent civilized peoples long divided unlocking possibility of...understanding."

Murmurs rippled around as she described the staggering archaeology proving cycles of rising mammal and mankind dominion guided by silent cosmic stewards. Gasps crescendoed as she revealed how modern technologies had accidentally cascaded the next era of intellectual beasts generations early.

"And we have all suffered from fear and chaos unleashed by this revelation..." Anna continued carefully. "But the coded past warns that reconciliation opens doors, while violence only breeds eternal stagnation. I propose a formal Concord to honor lost ages and weave a rich joint future that benefits all."

For endless moments, only the forest breeze stirred. Then slowly, powerfully, the great bear lord Ursus rose to all fours. "Your wisdom echoes the ancients, and we shall heed history's call. On this day, let our peoples be rejoined."

One by one, beasts, soldiers and chiefs alike rose in solemn accord. Harmony dawned on their horizon as Anna stood teary-eyed. Perhaps apocalypse could be averted and unexpected community birthed after all.

Chapter 33

THE MORNING DAWNED ominously through narrow gothic windows in the Parliament chamber. Reports had swelled of strange cyclones worsening coastal devastation as freak tides swallowed towns seemingly overnight. High alert echoed through the stone corridors as protective biohazard doors automatically sealed while emergency systems analyzed air samples for contamination.

Countless displaced species ambassadors huddled in the sealed halls anxiously communicating updates acrossrophic habitats and decimated migration channels worldwide. Food chain chaos had erupted in just days while no atmospheric or seismic cause surfaced to explain the violent worsening climate shifts.

When the doors finally opened signaling no contagion detected, Anna and Aurelius rushed through anxious crowds towards the United Wildlife Council's Situation Room buried beneath older human bunkers now adapted for interspecies threat coordination. Already visions loops played above the central table depicting junior diplomats rescued from wreckage across different disaster regions.

"Thank Gaia you both have arrived safely – we are only awaiting Supreme Chancellor Silvermane to activate Crisis Protocol," exclaimed the Humpback Whale Coordinator Busara straining telepathic communication over worsening storms interfering. "These simultaneous global events cannot be natural..."

As if hearing their summons, Chancellor Silvermane soon towered through reinforced security gates flanked by elite QRF response units bristling with tactical armor and specialized energy sensors. Their wise elder leader wasted no words as all turned towards displays highlighting accumulating damage reports and casualty projections shadowing doomsday models.

"Friends... if malicious origins orchestrate this siege upon the Earth itself then no faction disputes can compromise our response. Ready all Omega Protocol task forces at my order!"

Chapter 34

A SOBER ANXIETY WEIGHED upon the United Wildlife Council war room as Chancellor Silvermane and military generals coordinated rapid response to the deepening global environmental crisis. Entire coastal megacities now lay partially submerged while a perplexing cube structure was spotted emerging from receding Antarctic ice sheets.

"Our deepest scan satellites cannot penetrate this bizarre object's shell hovering over previously unknown complexes buried under the ice," explained General Revierre. "But we have confirmed non-biological properties before losing signal."

Silvermane nodded gravely as strange sigils reflecting off the levitating surfaces flashed across monitors. "And escalating seismic events offshore?"

"Indeed sir, and transmitting in odd harmonic wavelength patterns almost... ordering the extreme weather chains in syntax alignment," answered Busara the humpback telepath. "I am deciphering similar structures active in equatorial ocean ridges, Siberian tundra, and Gobi desert supercharging typhoon trajectories against habitat density gradients."

Like solar system security system activating after eons dormant, Anna realized with cold dread. Aurelius ruffled his feathers anxiously as cylcone diagnostics from Oceania wildlife aides highlighted unnatural plasma compression points. If alien defenses now perceived Earth's dominant crown compromised by ascended animal groups, would greater territorial sterilization protocols awaken?

"The message screams clear as a war siren to loose beasts now bound," General Revierre muttered. "Either the planet's godlike guardians reject our interspecies accords... or infinitely worse, some invisible enemy has taken over the fortresses intended to shelter peaceful life."

Chapter 35

A HEAVY GLOOM HUNG within the war room as Chancellor Silvermane's joint task forces raced to halt the weaponized global weather manipulating hidden alien structures now activated. Their own coastal cities lay half-submerged while bewildered urban families crowded emergency shelters.

"Have strike teams reached target zones surrounding the Antarctic monolith?" barked General Revierre. "We must gain operational control of these planetary defense matrices before irreversible climate decimation!"

Busara the whale telepath floated in her aquarium chamber, tendrils probing holograms of deep ocean sites. "Strike squads just breached several seafloor domes, no contacts yet... wait, I'm intercepting encrypted psychic shouts between sites warning of the raids!" Pairs of dolphins then swam urgently inside awaiting updates.

Meanwhile Aurelius studied reams of compiled folklore regarding the planet's absent caretaker species referenced across cultures. "Legends describe global generators harnessing geomagnetic currents towards... agricultural ends. Like irrigation controls for civilizational crops."

The Implications left Anna chilled. "If we've now been classified as a pestilent outbreak disrupting natural cycles after the Awakening breach, we face eradication by gardeners no longer recognizing humanity's sovereignty here..."

Just then, deafening alarms resounded as red warning glyphs swarmed tactical displays. Revierre swallowed hard addressing the chamber. "Strike teams just reported alien entities mobilizing to intercept at site perimeter defense grids. Chancellor - you have executive authority to engage."

Silvermane reared on powerful hind legs to tower over the assembly. "Then we shall fight for our peoples, our planet, and the Concord!" Determined bellows filled the hall. Claws, tentacles and fists raised with desperate hope against the coming storm.

Chapter 36

FLARES OF WEAPONS FIRE and shrieking war cries echoed through the muted chamber displays as Chancellor Silvermane and his senior strategists observed strike teams desperately battling alien entities across the decloaking planetary defense compounds. General Revierre barked orders dispatching reinforcements through shimmering portal gateways directly into raging firefights.

"Have Zulu Squad secured junction C-52 linking the Antarctic hub to Indian Ocean domes yet?" Silvermane demanded, his braided lion's mane bristling with combat hormones.

"Confirmed Junction C-52 now locked down, diverting power and isolating structure segments," reported General Singh, decorated Indian tigress. "But casualties are mounting with enemy technology far beyond our arsenal."

Displaying biometrics flashing distress beacons, Busara the whale telepath hovered in her aquatic chamber as dolphin aids worked security systems. "I'm interfacing through marine squadron minds now showing mortal wounds from the entity weapons. Their flesh seems to decay instantly as if a temporal disease..."

"By the gods, it's like fighting angry spirits!" Aurelius squawked. "Legends describe such vengeful custodians beyond our dimensional veil. We must strategize this occult assault before complete annihilation!"

Anna's mind raced applying analytical methods against the magical threats as casualties mounted horribly on screens. "There must be operational physics we can yet exploit! Everything breaks under precise conditions showing its design limits." Silvermane nodded solemnly before bellowing "Science units – identify structural weaknesses now or we perish this hour!"

Feverish minutes bled together as analytical teams urgently compiled data patterns revealed in raging crossfire through cracking alien domes. Anna gasped as revelations took form. "The plasma phase variance! It cycles every 4 minutes after each attack rotation!" Commanders roared coordinating final counterstrike waves for what little hope remained.

Chapter 37

BLARING KLAXONS RESOUNDED as the United Wildlife strike teams coordinated timing their assault on the vortex portal linking the weaponized alien structures harnessing catastrophic weather across the planet. General Revierre barked final orders from the war room for squadrons to target plasma condenser arrays during fluctuations in the energy cycle Anna's team identified.

"Strike force leaders – you have your operational windows and coordinates for surgical strikes on the vortex infrastructure! Breach points should be vulnerable every 4 minutes exactly." Revierre highlighted pulsating zones across the holographic displays from fresh intel packet updates.

Silvermane towered overhead conveying steely confidence now In their counterattack strategy, come what bloody may against the extraterrestrial threat. "On my signal, unleash unforgiving hell in united fury my friends! For earth and kin!" Rallying cheers rebounded across the chamber.

Moments crawled by on the digital clocks as tactical telemetry flooded mission control screens while squadrons went dark speeding into shielded alien structures through narrow access tunnels. Then finally a deafening blast sounded followed instantly by the entire vortex orb flickering wildly then dimming completely offline!

Manic shouts of victory erupted for long seconds before secondary explosions suddenly grenaded across all system visuals. Emergency bulkhead doors instantly descended while Busara screamed reports of sacrificial teams perishing inside from deadly counter-reactions. Austere silence then gripped the assembly witnesses the vengeful alien entities rematerializing like demons against their battered, outmatched

...strike teams

By Gaia and stars be damned, they've played their final card!"" Aurelius rasped solemnly. Silvermane lowered his crowned head muttering prayers for the ascended as slaughter howls echoed through chamber comms. Anna clenched her mentor's talons in solidarity until deafening white noise announced termination of all remaining forces. Total despair hung palpable with failure until an unnatural vibration

...resounded from deep below accompanied by blinding light

Chapter 38

A PROFOUND SILENCE engulfed the United WIldlife Council's war chamber following the devastating loss of their elite strike teams. Morale teetered dangerously even with enemy portal infrastructure now disabled. Harrowed faces still streamed tears while Chancellor Silvermane now lay on his side, weakened by sorrow and failure though .refusing to abandon leadership till his last labored breath

General Revierre stiffened suddenly then rushed to tactical monitors as alerts blared of massive energy displacement detected deep underground - directly below their most classified vaults warehousing powerful artifacts recovered from First Moon era sites dating to .forgotten beast dynasties

Seismic shockwaves still reverberating but signatures match no" earthly explosives..." Revierre reported with eyes narrowing. "I'm registering enormous neutrino and chronal particle transmission with "!bizarre quantum temporal readings

Heart catching realization, Anna grabbed Aurelius shouting. "The First Moon relics you showed me – this energy mirrors their spacetime manipulation properties from ancient lore! Could surviving beast monarchy allies be rallying some last asset we secured in secrecy?? It "!emanates straight from vault levels

With desperate hope rekindled, Silvermane heaved weighty limbs vertical again while tactical teams scrambled to access restricted vault cameras. Breathless minutes crawled by until feeds finally stabilized, displaying towering crystalline monoliths amidst the artifacts now glowing intensely bright while a shimmering temporal portal swirled ...violently before them. Then a towering silhouette slowly emerged Stepping into frame was perhaps the largest assemblage of fanged fangs and sinew they had witnessed. Eyes ancient yet annunciating ferocious purpose scanned the assembled war room through their camera feed. Lingering seconds passed before the colossal entity's snout peeled back unleashing an earth-shaking pronouncement in perfect :English

So too have forgotten epochs awakened new nightmares... But we"

"!shall finish what our descendants began

Chapter 39

BEWILDERED SHOCK RIPPLED through the United Wildlife
Council war room as the imposing beast demigod towering their
monitors bellowed his challenge against the marauding extraterrestrial
.entities still ambushing battered strike teams across the ravaged planet
General Revierre urgently cross-referenced surviving lore from
First Moon era artifacts describing mythical warrior saviors called
"Valkyries" who shepherded early mammals during prehistory.
Matching energy signatures and temporal readings now confirmed this
.giant newcomer's mythical Identity

Chancellor, unless my eyes fail me, scans match this warrior to"
archaicprphecies of great kings who defeat annihilating threats by
divine right!" Revierre exclaimed. "Biometric readings are off our charts
- I believe he possesses capacity to oppose the weaponized vortex
"!network

By Thor's thunder let it be true!" Silvermane answered pounding"
a mighty fist. He opened communications through prototype chronal
channels the science teams jury-rigged. "Brave leige, I am Supreme
Chancellor Silvermane. Will you champion our United Wildlife
"?Forces against this extinction-level invasion

The sound of entire ancient forests crashing down resounded as the
Valkyrie commander flexed stone-cracking muscle before thundering
his proclamation. "I AM ASGARD, FIRST FATHER TO THE
MAMMAL NOBLES NOW FACING EXTIRPATION! BY MY

BLOOD OATH, NONE SHALL THREATEN MY HEIRS WHILE BREATH REMAINS. COME THEN DIVINE "!GENOCIDER – FACE RAGNAROK

A deafening roar shook the chamber as monitors tracked the Valkyrie warlord bursting topside through reinforced levels before engaging antigravity thrusters towards the nearest alien artifact dome. "All strike squadrons still combat effective, rendezvous on Asgard for assault on vortex core!" ordered General Revierre. Perhaps salvation .existed on this dire hour before apocalypse after all

Their screens soon filled with scenes of savage close-quarters warfare waged in the belly of the colossal alien generators. At long last, !with earth's secret prince unleashed, hope burned again

Chapter 40

CAUSTIC SMOKE PLUMED from shattered alien domes as Chancellor Silvermane observed vicious close-quarters battle raging within the vortex portal complex on tactical monitors. Having smashed his way inside the central core structure, the mythical beast warrior Asgard now plowed through horrifically outmatched strike teams with uncontrolled fury towards his genocidal foes.

General Revierre highlighted forthcoming chronal energy spikes predicted from the destabilizing portal as United Wildlife forces fought desperately to hold junction chokepoints. "Temporal currents are wildly erratic - we're detecting enormous neutrino buildup converging on Asgard's position!!"

Heart seizing as screens illuminated the Valkyrie conqueror's bio-aura shining stellar bright amidst the fray, Anna screamed. "Chancellor the portal cannot handle his cosmic radiation output! If he unleashes full fury we'll have uncontrolled black hole collapse taking Earth with it!"

"By my father's gray mane... we must extract Asgard before catastrophe despite his crusade!" Silvermane slammed emergency orders to full retreat just as the vagrant warrior let loose a cataclysmic overhead fist that exploded spacetime Itself. Alarms drowned all channels moments before screens went fully static then blinked out permanently.

Deafening minutes crawled by only interrupted by panicked calls from orbiting stations that Earth's gravitational flux was spiraling deadly erratic! Aurelius muttered choked prayers until Busara suddenly cried out clutching her temples. "The global weather anomalies are "!dissolving rapidly – I'm tuning wavelength Irregularities fading As desperate emergency teams worked to reroute observation Inbound, Anna squeezed Aurelius close daring fragile hope as Silvermane stood silent awaiting visual proof. Finally a blurry aerial visual link stabilized, revealing colossal alien structures rubble and smoking debris...yet atmosphere readings normalized! Against all odds, they had narrowly swerved armageddon's head-on crash. Weary sighs .shook the chamber at prospects of securing lasting peace

Chapter 41

A bright new dawn rose over the battered capital cityscape still showing scars but stabilized from nature's wrath. Inside emergency parliament chambers, Chancellor Silvermane stood flanked by his diverse interspecies council members as crowds gathered expectantly around giant monitors erected outside.

"My friends, no words can convey the sacrIfice so many made resisting extinction's grip so that we may endure," Silvermane began, voice heavy with sorrow for martyrs. "Today we stand not just as individuals but a collective civilization who together faced liberation's twilight hour.

"For it was only by the bravery shown across tribes, and wisdom embracing our shared destiny, that salvation prevailed even when oblivion's shadows drew closest." Moved murmurs rippled amongst the assembly. Anna spotted not a dry eye.

"Of course a steep road awaits rebuilding, yet now we walk it imbued with deeper bonds those survival fires forged. Let our renewed unity stand as a monument shining hope towards unborn generations

A breathless aura swelled within the chamber as Aurelius stepped forward raising a crystal chalice. "To life eternal and spirits who shepherded fate's wheel towards continuity. So too may our ListedColormap thrive forever In hard-won harmony – both strength "!and fragility woven as one

Rapturous cheers erupted through the parliament as crowds outside took up a cathartic chant blessing their united world. And gazing across the diversity of muzzles, beaks and faces overflowing with hope renewed, Anna knew that whatever fresh sunrise mysteries still .await over the horizon, for now lasting peace had dawned for good .No matter tomorrow's unknowns, they stood ready for the light

Chapter 42

"INCOMING STARGATE TRANSMISSION from Alpha Centauri" domain, Lieutenant!" chirped the decorative cockatoo aid perched intently before fluctuating monitors. "Shall I buffer the diplomatic "?overture for your nest-mother the Strategic Director to review

Lieutenant Amer Bahir smiled affectionately at his avian assistant Tikki – one of the new interspecies administrative generations hatched across the capital since the vortex invasion that nearly spelt doom before revolutionary Concord agreements averted genocidal calamity .years prior

I believe Director Zahra should indeed assess this latest" extraterrestrial contact given recent tensions," Amer answered, brushing pale vitiligo spots dotting his rich skin as he analysed galactic protocol scans. "Prioritize priority channel encryption as alwayss per ".unity security protocols

Ever since a disastrous first contact incident with the hostile alien vortex entities escaping isolated captivity on a Martian outpost, joint human-beast United Planetary Leadership took precautions managing extraterrestrial diplomatic relations. But Major Bahir had faith their strengthened alliance could persevere against external threats just as

...their heroic predecessors achieved decades ago on Earth

As little Tikki rapidly translated the incoming Centauri message through several xenolinguistic cyphers, Amer reviewed classified files recently decrypted from the prehistoric First Moon era. Some hinted at

83

ancient pacts with celestial stewards who seeded stabilized planets like primitive Earth with caretaker colonies eons past. Were these mythic progenitors still guiding interstellar alliances across the galaxies even today?

A confident chirp interrupted Amer's woolgathering - Tikki had decoded the essential meaning now from their alien transmission. Earth had been invited to a major interplanetary consortium discussing unified responses to an unusual cosmic radiation spike detected...

Chapter 43

LIEUTENANT BAHIR STRODE swiftly through the bustling United Planetary Defense Force headquarters, glancing occasionally at the holographic windows displaying real-time traction of their diplomatic envoy vessels en route toward the Centauri Consortium assembly. He pressed his palm against the access pad entering the Strategic Director's chamber.

"Director Zahra, the first contact delegation has successfully translated to non-relativistic speeds nearing the Centauri rendezvous point," Amer reported with a sharp salute. "Their last status update indicates significant military Infrastructure mobilizing however – possibly a show of force."

The décorated Egyptian Mau feline warrior nodded from her elevated post. "A cautious prospect indeed. We must take care that overzealous fleet commanders do not provoke unnecessary engagements. Have CaptaIn Saidi emphasize our unified planetary banner during approach."

"At once ma'am," Amer acknowledged while reviewing the diverse coalition now representing Earth'shybrid interests abroad for the first time. Advanced cetacean navigators guided their diplomatic frigate fleet relying on quantum chronal engine arrays reverse-engineered from First Moon era technology. Alongside stood seasoned Sasquatch commanders directing tactical teams comprised of both awakened hawks and macaques wielding non-lethal plasma shields. Peace was priority one, yet vigilance essential in unpredictable galaxies.

Approaching Centauri space stations orbiting splendorous bronze-hued planets, the lead United Planet envoys transmitted harmonious greetings species-wide through lunar wavelength channels specifically. Minutes passed awaiting responses. Finally, their monitors flickered with incoming images of an intimidating bipedal race resembling hybrid reptilian warriors outfitted for interplanetary war...

The Centauri commander's slit eyes narrowed assessing the Earth delegation led by a uniformed lion warrior and blue whale Admiral. His translated galactic common tongue carried harsh vowels. "We received your crafts' gravitational echoes. What now stirs the humility of feral Earth to finally reach beyond your nesting burrows?"

Director Zahra leaned forward intensely evaluating the delicate opening dialogue. Her whiskers bristled guessing these draconian Centauri likely respected only shows of strength. Perhaps peaceful integration into the stars would require awakening further old world fangs and cunning...

Chapter 44

A TENSE SILENCE HUNG over the United Planetary embassy vessels as the reptilian Centauri delegation continued scrutinizing the joint human-beast emissaries representing a newly unified Earth. Admiral Kshama, senior cetacean officer, initiated secondary translation attempts broadcasting goodwill.

"We humbly navigate these stars under banner of interspecies cooperation following historic age of turmoil now reconciled within expanding horizon, honored Centauri..." she transmitted through lyric marine patterns. "Yet still have far voyages toward enlightenment ahead together should open trust bloom between our peoples..."

The Centauri commander tilted his angular head assessing the whale's beamed codes before grunting in his native tongue. "Nautilus mind-talker, we decoded your liquid thoughts. But what worth offers your mismatched horde to mighty Draconis order? Prove yourselves beyond savage dichotomy through respectable sacrifice, then earned respect may come."

Director Zahara discreetly extended honed claws judging the harsh Centauri terms. Faster-than-light travel opportunities would greatly accelerate their united planet's ascension into the galaxies as an equal power if they could gain access through this starfaring race. Would old instincts to dominate rather than compromise now compromise delicate aspirations for interplanetary harmony just beyond grasp?

The lead Sasquatch ambassador Chayton reading Zahara's pensive cues lumbered forward next wielding initiation totems. "By code woven into our common fabric, all may meet illuminated. Thus we present this gift in hope of seeding mutual soils under star patterns familiar to all seekers."

He offered an ornate crystalline skull with flickering nebula energy strata eerily reminiscent of vortex technologies that once brought Earth civilizations to near extinction. The Centauri delegates leaned closer intrigued by the pulsating offering...

What happened next passed in mere seconds yet somehow stretched lifetimes. Blinding neutrino sparks erupted from the skull matrix, engulfing all present in pure light as haunting echoes called from deep space. United Planet crew members reported feeling eternity embrace their life flames instantaneously...as hidden galactic archives whispered awakening guidance.

Chapter 45

ADMIRAL KSHAMA SLOWLY awoke finding herself inexplicably in an alien cryostasis chamber as null gravity distorted all senses. Telepathically shouting through fluid tanks, her delphine aids reported entire United Planet crews similarly locked in stasis across vast ship bays. No Centauri guards responded to desperate queries until agenda behind their paralysis became clear...

Med scanners tracking deep space vital signs soon relayed chilling updates – diplomatic fleet navigation showed reckless course deviation directly into the Cygnus quasar formation! Reason overrode panic as Kshama calculated just 8 standard hours now before absorption into the massive plasma accretion disks disintegrated all vessels if trajectories held...

Director Zahara awoke restrained by biomechanical tendrils linking her chamber to an alien hivemind apparently simulating tactical outcomes of various invasion scenarios targeting Earth's weakened biosphere defenses. Horrified realizing the diplomatic overture had been an elaborate ruse for conquest, Zahara activated code red psionic pulses ordering all crew telepaths to target connection nodes for shutdown. But interfaced Centauri minds quickly retaliated by threatening to choke cryo-held hostages!

On the expansive bridge, Chayton the lead sasquatch envoy stirred sealed inside a diagnostic cylinder prodded by laser analysis beams mapping his genome for vulnerabilities. Through the glass walls, reptilian researchers observed as a disembodied alien computer voice stated: "Cross-species hybridization program now initiating Gestalt sequence. Standby for complete neural override..."

Alarmed by implications, Chayton braced for invasive reprogramming and silently urged his captive crew toward courage as the quasar loomed...

Chapter 46

ALARMS BLARED WITHIN the cryostasis bay as Admiral Kshama and her telepathic marine staff desperately strategized countermeasures before their hijacked diplomatic fleet reached the deadly Cygnus quasars. But with most crew neurologically paralyzed, options were starkly limited.

In the genetics laboratory, Chayton choked back nausea as the Centauri Gestalt hivemind excruciatingly unpacked his genetic memories seeking means to exploit crossspecies weaknesses for invasion goals. Just when psychic tension screamed unendurable, the sasquatch shaman retreated into transcendent mindfulness, adopting oneiric techniques used by ancestors for aeons untold.

Instantly Chayton found himself traversing trippy dreamscapes beyond physical existence where cosmic consciousness flows unchecked by dimensions. As worlds blurred, his essence interwove all surrounding lifeforms and quantum particles across both distant galaxies and subatomic layers into taprooted unity. For a timeless instant, all existence breathed as singular whole through perspectives infinite...

Abruptly the vivid vision collapsed as electric jolts erupted inside Chayton's holding cylinder. Alarms shrieked as automated quarantine sealed the genetics lab. Burst coolant pipes obscured sight but through icy fog Chayton glimpsed the lead Centauri researcher typing furiously then shouting orders for immediate data purge before more arcane contagion spread!

Moments later emergency bulkheads unsealed as hazmat teams extracted a disoriented Chayton now clothed and gesturing wildly about the dreamtime revelation. Apparently his transcendent shamanic breakout had cascaded unprecedented systemic psychic overflow the Gestalt couldn't compartmentalize, sparking ship-wide temporary shutdown!

As cryo-thaw revival commenced fleetwide, Chayton knew more radically unbounded tactics held their hope now. The cosmos called for mystics and warriors alike heeding destiny's song...

Chapter 47

AS THE LIBERATED DIPLOMATIC fleet fires full velocity away from Centauri oppressors, Director Zahara convenes an emergency summit of commanding officers in the war room. Still reeling from close catastrophe, shocked faces try processing the implications of narrowly dodging conquest while armed now with revelation of a larger interstellar conflict raging secretly across inhabited galaxies. Zahara pounds a fist, demanding bold strategy proposals to shift the tide in Earth's volatile favor...

Meanwhile on Mars, the excavation team led by Dr. Horace uncovers a luminescent alien egg preserved in ancient permafrost that begins rapidly incubating from exposure. Scans note astonishing complexity unlike anything matching terrestrial or even Centauri biology. As it starts mysteriously pulling data from all networked systems nearby, Horace contacts old colleague Anna from the beast awakening era for her expertise. They must urgently unlock secrets before this hatching extraterrestrial menace potentially triggers more world-shaking upheaval....

When Anna's transport ship stops for reflective solitude on Europa's icy exterior en route, she suddenly receives a faint repeating radio transmission from... a small dog frantically digging itself free of age-old frozen nitrogen near a wrecked NASA surface rover! Rescuing the cryo-preserved canine revives painful memories that resignation can't keep buried. For fate now offers second chances if the courage still remains to try as epochal cycles churn anew...

Chapter 48

A NERVOUS ENERGY PERCOLATES within the United Planetary Defense Force headquarters as Admiral Kshama urgently translates intercepted Centauri battle comm chatter detailing invasion fleets massing lightyears away. Director Zahara assembles top generals to analyze attack projections based on their prior vulnerability breach.

"By the eternal tide's turn, we must spirItually unlock survival instincts to resist extinction before true diplomacy may bloom..." Kshama sings somberly through the war room speakers. "Our weeping mothers once faced such calamity and overcame through unity's grace."

This haunting reminder of the near-apocalypse triggered by First Moon era forces generations ago crystallizes Zahara's realization - more martial cunning alone cannot win tomorrow's wars. True victory, just as their ancestors achieved, requires awakening ancient psychological lineage linking all who navigate the abyss.

"You speak wisdom, Admiral," Zahara replies while activating the genome archives. "If beast and mankind jointly dispelled vortex threats by reconciling past, present and possibility, so too must we synthesize a fighting spirit prepared for advancing eras!"

As the council explores reconciling interspecies divisions amongst their personnel, Zahara makes contact with Alpha Centauri refugees that fled after the draconian regime seized power. Hidden settlement coordinates are exchanged as the rebels represent vital alliance opportunities...

Concurrently on Mars, Dr. Horace watches astonished as the decoded alien egg absorbs all surrounding energy to fuel exponentially accelerating incubation. Desperate for answers, he establishes contact with Anna's transport still days away. They confer on astonishing device energy signatures suggesting links to the mysticalCygnus anomaly revealed during first contact! If true, was this a deus ex machina... or ?doomsday countdown

Chapter 49

ENCRYPTED STARSHIP rendezvous coordinates arrive initiating Director Zahara's off-books mission meeting Alpha Centauri resistance commandos that fought the draconian regime plaguing United Planet hopes. Slipping past flesh-hungry nebula storms, she lands at towering ruins scanned as matching First Moon ancestry.

There Zahara's team is greeted by an advanced bipedal race evolved from Earth's raptor dynasties according to encoded genetic data. Apparently, Cygnus light burst sent various mammalian and reptilian genetic seeds across galaxies eons ago – spawning both familiar and unrecognizable civilized breeds like these Raptorians allied against tyranny. Some still safeguard primordial archives detailing the mythic chrono-crystalline technologies that decide ascendance...

Impatient for Anna's wisdom facing threats on two planetary fronts now, Horace scans the hyper-encrypting alien egg calculating mere days remain before a staged incubation Phase Shift. Desperate for assistance, he hastily dons an inverse ion radiation suit crafted by his sentient Rover bot then manually enters the active energy sphere protecting the species-undefined embryo...

Floating through cascading chronometric particles revealing timespace impressions from lightyears away, Horace is shocked recognizing galactic scenes of draconian assault battalion strikes against defensive strongholds. Peering closer at their Raptorian resistance targets, Horace's heart skips witnessing insignia-markings identical to some hatching before him on Mars! Direct ancestry cannot be random if technology so advanced...

With mixed hope and terror as the egg grows charged for full emergence, Horace ponders how to handle astonishing life bearing traces across the stars and eras of Earth's intertwined destiny...

Chapter 50

AWASH WITH AWE IN EUROPA'S deep translucent caverns beholding an ancient beast king preserved cryogenically since disaster ended his era untold millennia ago, Anna initializes resuscitation schematics on her wrist interfaces based on First Moon biotech archives. As her lost dog Clyde observes suspiciously, gas bubbles erupt from the liquified glacier cocoon. Years after gifting that tragic canine soul renewed purpose, Anna braces to perhaps come full circle in her ...own understanding

Lightyears beyond, Director Zahara and her Alpha Centauri Raptorian Special Ops squad decrypt critical intel pinpointing vulnerabilities in Centaurii planetary blockade formations utilizing illegally hybridized neurotech developed on a captured earth scientist. Outraged hearing Subcommander Iris identifies the human collaborator as former United Nations polecat attaché Dr. Luka Dubcek seeking to regain animal authority with invasive brain hack implants, Zahara demands Immediate retrieval and tribunal for the ...traitor

Meanwhile inside Mars cryo-containment, lead researcher Dr. Horace explores virtual summary interface encoded on the hyper-reactive alien egg's surface presented as its gestation climax nears activation in two martian solar cycles. Desperately absorbing untranslated data context aroundPhoenix glyphs representing imminent Phase Shift events, Horace prays Anna's wisdom may

decipher foreboding unIversal triggers across eons suggestIng this new
...progeny's role deciding evolutionary tracts of multiple worlds
Settling into temporary shared habitat quarters aboard the
Raptorian stealth cruiser Lightseeker bound for blockaded Centauri
borders, decorated Egyptian Mau commander Zahara watches
Paleoceneosaurian engineers conduct final system tests for their secret
chrono-shift weapon stowed near converted antique terrestrial Rosetta
data gold discs packed with linguistic primers. Destiny hangs balanced
...between eras

Chapter 51

AMBER STASIS FLUID pulses then drains rapidly as Anna, Clyde and modern beast generals intently support cryo-emergence of long-hibernating animalia monarch Mammut the Mammoth from glacial resurrection. Ancient eyes brightening again under the européan moon, Mammut trumpets explosively before locking tusks with Clyde embracing the fellow mammal pioneer displaced across lost epochs. Emotions surge witnessing extinct magnificence reborn into

...importance once more

Lightyears beyond Mars, Raptorian planet-class dreadnoughts uncloak unleashing temporal displacement spheres that shift the Centauri fleet flagships out of combat phase moments before they trigger doomsday chronal weapons. The enemy armada hangs motionless as Director Zahara's strike teams led by turncoat Dr. Dubcek seize navigation controls through the paralysis effect. On her command, the co-opted ships' plasma drives are set to Implode

...containing the time-frozen threat as crews evacuate

In the ensuing calm aboard Mars colony Ark, Horace urgently reviews Centauri battle footage transmitted from Zahara's victory with Anna & awakened Mammut analyzing implications around the alien egg counting down to hatching. They confirm its incubation perfectly mirrors previous dominant species phase shift emergence aligned to Cygnus energy gifts. This rare future-sculpting child must be shielded

...from militaristic exploitation

Hours later as the triplicate suns align for conception, the Mars colony witnesses astonishing chromatic rays bathe the red landscape as the mysterious egg fractures. While human scientists observe reverently, mobile forces lower armaments In deference to new life. And arising joyfully from Its prototypes across galaxies comes a wondrous crystalline avian Savior – benign quintessence of unity's light beaming far brighter than mere dominance, promising cooperative

.civilizations secured

Mammut trumpets proudly seeing already buried chronotech ancestry manifested again for this budding age. All present organisms sense rebirth's longer arc now winding surely through silently watching stars and ancient Mammut's gleaming eyes full of hope for generations

...imperiled no more

About the Author

Hadi Hans is an aspiring young author who draws upon his rich life experiences in his writing ,Imarried with two lovely daughters named Lucine and Lorianne.

Hadi continues traveling extensively to fuel his literary passions, and draws daily inspiration from his diverse surroundings.

His rich global upbringing informs his empathy-driven stories.

desire to bridge divides between people via storytelling. His experiences grant authentic perspectives to his fiction.

The dream has always been to write books for children and adults as well.